Rose's Diary

Olwyn Harris

Published by: Reading Stones Publishing
Helen Brown & Wendy Wood
Woodwendy1982.wixsite.com/readingstones
Cover Design: Olwyn Harris

For more copies contact the publisher at:

Glenburnie
212 Glenburnie Road
ROB ROY NSW 2360
Mobile: 0422 577 663
Email: Readingstonespublishing@gmail.com

Dedication:
To Kate – my own princess who told me this parable was her favourite story and it changed her life.

Once upon a time there was a beautiful princess. She loved sitting in her fragrant rose garden, listening to her golden canary sing his heart out. However, the princess did not spend all her time lingering in her garden. She worked hard at learning to be the best princess she could be. She studied her books on how to govern a kingdom and learnt about money, trade, bookkeeping, and politics. She listened to the Kingdom diplomats as they diplomatically made Kingdom decisions. She learnt her lessons well.

Then one day her father, the king, summoned her. "Beautiful daughter", he said, "I have watched you study hard and learn from many books. You have a head for the things needed to run a kingdom, such as diplomacy and politics. But before a princess is appointed to an official position of responsibility, there is another lesson to be learnt. I want you to investigate what it is to be one of your subjects."

Another lesson did not sound too difficult to the princess. She was not only beautiful, but clever as well. Already in her mind the princess started to calculate how to research this project. She began to formulate survey questions to target sample population groups. But the King quietly held up his regal hand. "I want you to dress as one of the common people and live in the village. For a time you will be treated like one of them."

"But Father!" exclaimed the Princess in shock. "I am the princess royal. Everyone will know it is I. They will treat me differently."

"If you are able to stay in the village until I come to summon you home, you will be ready to be appointed to a position of great responsibility. I will see that you have everything you need to fulfil this assignment, but the people are not to know you that are the princess royal."

The princess went away quite confused. This lesson sounded more difficult than any one project she had ever done before. How she wished she could just write a clever essay about the village. She could write an essay quickly, but to *live* in the village would take time – possibly a long time! She didn't think it was a very good idea. She went back to the King. But he refused to see her. He told his royal messenger, "My daughter, the princess, is away on a special assignment. Anyone who claims to be the Princess Royal would surely be an impostor! I will not see them! One warning: if they come again, there will be severe and terrible punishment for impersonating a royal personage."

The princess knew she had no choice but to complete the assignment. She called her servants to pack her royal bags. She called them again. No one came. She was very angry at their tardiness and went looking for them. They were busy doing other important things for the King. They did not seem to notice she was there. She called for her royal carriage. The carriage driver listened patiently to the beautiful princess and then said, "His Majesty, my Royal Highness the King, has personally decreed that his carriages only be brought out for his private use. I cannot take you anywhere."

"But I am only doing what he asked me to do. It is a most difficult task. I need a royal carriage."

"You cannot use a carriage. I do not doubt that the King in his wisdom believes you have everything you need to complete his directions already."

The princess went back to her royal quarters and decided to pack her royal bags herself. But when she went to her royal closet, everything was gone, except two clean, plain, brown peasant's dresses, an apron, one journal, and five coins. She changed her dress and wrapped the journal in the apron and walked out of the palace into the village.

* * *

Peasant Life

The princess went to the inn and asked for a room. The innkeeper looked at her strangely, and said, "Our fee is one coin a week. There is a cheaper lodging house down the street." The princess nearly told the man that he had no right to refuse her lodging because she was the beautiful princess royal. But as she thought about her five coins, she realised that soon she would run out of money if she did not think carefully. She thanked him humbly and went down the street to the cheaper lodge. The house was dirty, and the food did not smell very good, but it used only one of her coins for three weeks lodging, and that gave her time to think.

She sat down on the bed and opened the journal. On the front page was an inscription that said:

"To my dearest daughter,

May the lessons you learn

bring more wisdom

than all the learning from many books.

~ from your beloved Father."

Tears welled up in her beautiful eyes. If her father loved her as well as he said, why would he ask such a thing? Perhaps he was not her father after all. Perhaps this was a way to get rid of her. Never in all her short, pampered life had the princess felt so abandoned and alone. That night she cried herself to sleep.

In the morning, she awoke when dusty rays of morning sun streamed through the broken shutters onto her bunk. She called to her servants to bring her breakfast; but then she remembered what her life had become. She dressed alone and sat thinking. One thought kept coming to her mind. The first line of the inscription in her diary: "To my dearest daughter." If she really believed those words, it meant her father had not disowned her. She remembered her father's gentle voice as he told her what he wanted her to do. She realised she did indeed believe those words. Soon he would summon her home, and she could go back to her father and hand her diary over to him and say: "I have completed the task you set before me, Father." She would trust his wisdom. She would choose to have confidence that he knew what was best for her and his subjects. All at once she knew she would need to draw on every lesson she ever had, to learn what it meant to be a royal subject in their province.

The beautiful princess knew she needed to find a job so she would have money to live on. She opened her diary and wrote in the date. *"Today"*, she wrote, *"I begin my journey. I have taken the name 'Rose'. The sweet-smelling blooms in the garden at home are my favourite memory."*

She went out in search for a position. She knocked at a door. "Hello," she said, "my name is Rose. I am looking for a job."

The lady of the house looked at her clean dress and smooth hair sceptically and asked, "Hmmm? What can ya do?"

"Do?" asked Rose.

"Yeah. What do ya *do?*"

"Ummm," Rose thought quickly. She couldn't say that she could cook – because she couldn't. She couldn't sew because the royal seamstress always made her royal gowns. She could hardly say she was competent at royal bookkeeping and political science – because they wouldn't understand. In the end she just sighed and said, "Nothing."

"I don't need *nothing* done!" said the woman and shut the door.

Rose went to the next house and the next. She never thought that it would be difficult to engage a position. She assumed only lazy people didn't work. At night she went back to the dingy Inn. Her dress was dirty from the dusty, filthy streets and her legs ached from walking all day. She opened her diary and wrote. *"Today I looked for a position. But I don't know how to cook or do laundry. I have to be able to do something for them."* She turned to the back of her diary and wrote on the page: '*civil sanitation*', and under that she wrote, '*employment*'.

The next day she continued her quest... and the next. Finally, she came to a house where a distraught mother came to the door, dark circles under her eyes, rocking a flushed, crying baby. "What'd ya want?" she asked impatiently. Rose started her speech, but she stopped. "I want to help," she said quietly.

The mother was taken aback. "Why?" she asked.

Rose said simply, "I have nothing else to do today," and she thought she could look for a job tomorrow.

The mother opened up the door. "If ye mean it, I am grateful. I have nothing to pay ye. My husband died in a blacksmithing accident. Come in and see what ye can do."

Rose looked around in despair. In truth she did not know what she could do. Four wide-eyed urchins looked hungrily from the floor under the table. There was junk and clutter around, so Rose gingerly started to take the rubbish outside. Then she cleared the table and opened up the shutters to let in some light and fresh air. She asked the mother for directions and went and got some water from the stagnant village pond, to wash the bench table. Then she scrubbed the children's little faces until their cheeks glowed red.

They only had a few potatoes for food. Rose looked at them. "How do you cook your potatoes?" she asked the mother who sat despondently rocking her sick babe.

"I boil them... but I have run out of fuel for my stove."

"Oh." Rose paused. If she used her money to buy fuel, she would have nothing to eat herself, and how would that help? "Is there another way?"

The lady sighed. "Of course – if you have fuel... you can fry and roast, and scallop and fritter and mash and bake or even make stew and soup ... but what is the use? I have no fuel. It was different when my husband was alive and worked his blacksmith shop. My babies had plenty of food."

Rose thought. "What is your favourite way to cook potatoes, Peggie?" she asked the mother.

"Fried. I have a little laird left, but no bread to put it on."

Rose went down the street to a house that had smoke coming from the chimney. She asked for some live coals from their fire and took them back to the house. She set them under the pile of rubbish outside. She got a pan and the laird and cut the potatoes. The rubbish was smoky and smelly as it burnt, but the potatoes started to sizzle and soon they were cooking. The children ate their potatoes hungrily.

Eventually, Rose sat down and offered to hold the crying infant while Peggie ate. She held it like a prickly porcupine. Peggie quickly took the baby back. "She is sick and won't settle for anyone else," she said apologetically. Then she looked at Rose. "You ain't done this before – have ye?"

Rose blushed. Did she guess who she was? What would she do if she failed in her assignment? "No – but I want to learn to help."

"Ye have helped... just by being here."

Rose went back to her room at the lodging house. She could not get Peggie and her little children out of her mind. She opened her diary and wrote: "*I miss many things... my clothes, my canary, my assistants, my roses, my books, but most of all I miss having control. There are things here over which I have no control.*" In the back of her book, she wrote: '*winter fuel*', and '*health care*'.

The next day she went back to Peggie. "I will pay for a doctor to see baby Lottie,"

Tears came to Peggie's eyes. "I don't understand why you would want to help."

"You have been kind to me Peggie. I just want to see your family safe."

Rose paid for the doctor. She had only two weeks lodging left. She desperately needed to do something so she could pay for a room and food to eat, before her money ran out. She kept looking for a job.

* * *

After a few days she went back to see baby Lottie. She was a little better, but the family still looked hungry. Peggie smiled when she saw Rose. They sat down and talked together. Suddenly Rose said, "Did you say your husband owned a blacksmith shop?"

"Yes, but there is no one to work it. My father-in-law is old and frail. He lives with his daughter, and her husband's family has always worked in the Royal Stables. My husband has no brothers. My son is too young to learn the trade. His tools lie unused. I thought about selling them, but I cannot part with them yet. Perhaps one day, I will be hungry enough."

Slowly Rose looked about her. "It is a shame that your husband's legacy sits dormant when it could provide for his family now."

Peggie looked at this stranger who had come out of nowhere with offers to help. "You don't know what you are saying. I have five young children to look after!"

"I do not expect you to work the shop, but perhaps there is someone else who can do blacksmithing from the village."

"No. The work is sent to the next village now. They have a large shop there."

"Is there no master around who could work the forge?" asked Rose.

"My father-in-law knows the skills, but he does not have the strength to do the work. I don't know of anyone else."

"If we could find someone to do the work – would you be willing to open the shop again?"

Peggie grimaced. "Yes," she said simply.

Rose offered to help Peggie manage the shop. She sat down and made some calculations. She drew up a business plan and projected seasonal cost and profit estimates. But it all depended on finding a strong, willing man to learn off the frail old master. She went back through the village and knocked on the doors. "Hello," she said, "my name is Rose. I am looking to employ a person." She explained what she wanted but no one was willing to release their son. It was unorthodox to suggest working outside allotted professions. One lady told her it was a ridiculous idea: her family had only ever been millers. Another man declared his son would always be a tailor. Most said their men were working the fields for the King.

Finally, Rose came upon two willing candidates: one was a village outcast: a poor illegitimate man named Fillip who collected rags and bones for a living; the other was a stranger to the village who had taken a room in the boarding house. Rose and Peggie outlined the terms of the apprenticeship, and they both made their mark on the line.

Under the eye of the master, Rose helped clean out the disused shop behind Peggie's house. Fillip got up early and did his garbage collection rounds before he started in the blacksmith shop. He knew where to collect fuel and would bring enough back to the shop every morning so the forge-work could begin. Their first job was to make a comfortable chair for the old man to sit in as he tutored his novice smiths.

Rose went through the village and told the people they didn't need to send their blacksmithing jobs to the next village anymore. Few were willing to risk it. They did not want to entrust their ploughs to a stranger or an inexperienced, illegitimate rag and bone man. But sometimes they were stuck and needed the wheel fixed on their cart in a hurry or wanted a new axe head, or a link in a chain mended towards the end of the day.

They worked hard, and saved their money so Fillip could buy an old horse and a dilapidated cart for his rag and bone rounds. He fixed up the cart and even with an old horse he could complete his rounds more quickly. He had more time to work the forge as the jobs came in and eventually Fillip hired a young lad to help with the garbage rounds.

Rose was often in the shop. She helped Peggie understand how to keep records of jobs in a book. Peggie asked Rose to stay at their hut, so they could work together at night after the children were in their bunks. They would order supplies, receipt the payments of jobs and wages. Peggie's husband had always managed these things, but Peggie was an astute woman and was determined that her children would not suffer.

The stranger from the boarding house got restless and left, but Fillip continued learning. His arms became skilled as he hammered iron on the anvil. He was used to hard, dirty work, and he found the old man interesting to listen to. Other travelling strangers started blacksmithing with Fillip, but again and again they got tired, or bored, or frustrated, or angry... and left Fillip and the Master to struggle on alone. Until one day Mark came, cap in hand, asking for work with a foreign accent.

When Rose learned Mark was another itinerant from the boarding house she nearly said "no" to his request for a job. But the workload had begun to increase as the villagers entrusted more jobs to their workshop. She needed another person to help Fillip. She remembered her first day in the village as an outsider and promised to give him the opportunity to prove himself. He already knew some things about iron and the forge and was eager to learn more.

Little Lottie and the other children would run in and out of the racks and tools, laughing and playing with Fillip if he was not very busy. He would quietly pick Lottie up, if she wandered near the hot forge and tickle her tummy before he set her down to play in another area of the shop.

Peggie always said, "Thank you for your hard work, Fillip," before they left.

He always responded, "You are welcome. It helps us both."

Peggie shared her meagre allowance with Rose to cover their basic needs. They now had enough money to buy flour from the Miller and they bought extra coal as they could afford it and sold it to the villagers for a few extra pennies. They could buy potatoes and started a small vegetable garden of their own. In the corner of the garden, Rose planted a rose bush... one that had beautiful pink roses, and some mornings when it was quiet she would wake up early and sit there, listening to the sparrows chirp good morning, and the ducks quack as they splashed in the puddles. During the day she helped the children carry water from the village pond to water their garden and she always made sure that they boiled the water before they drank it. Peggie would take freshly baked buns to her father-in-law to share with Fillip and Mark as they worked.

Rose went to her bed in the corner of the loft. She had not written in her diary for a long time. She wrote: *"Peggie's Blacksmith shop is working again. I am teaching her basic numbers and letters to help her manage the shop. The business is gaining credibility and Fillip is learning well. Mark is an enigma. He has stayed longer than the others from the boarding house. He always works hard, but his heart is not in the craft like Fillip. I suspect he will leave soon – just like the others. I will look again for another young apprentice from the village to start. Now that the shop is more established there may be interest. I am concerned about the village water. Drinking the dirty water is not safe. There is a lot of sickness in the village. We need a well that will provide fresh water that is not used for washing laundry or watering cows or as a playground for ducks."*

She turned to the back of her diary and wrote: 'education' and 'a village well'.

* * *

Lost

Rose waited for the call of her Father. Every morning she had looked out the window in the loft and wondered if this was the day her Father would call her back to the palace. She waited. She worked. She waited and waited... and the more she waited, the easier it was just to work. Rose became so used to the grime of the workshop that it was easy to forget she was once the pampered only daughter of the Kingdom's sovereign. It was easier to throw herself into the life of a villager and pretend this was the way it has always been. She missed her privileges, and she missed her golden canary. The chirping of the brown, dull sparrows did offer a little comfort as she watched them hop around on the pavement, but nothing here made beautiful music like her canary. Even though they had as much coal as they needed to supply the village now, the dirty, grimy layers of coal dust that settled over her clothes reminded Rose of what village life was like: dirty, confined and basic. The crowded corner in the cottage filled with noisy, crying children, became her home.

Finally, she realised that her father did not truly intend to call her back. His aim was to lose his daughter after all. That night she cried herself to sleep again and then the next morning Rose tucked her diary under her dusty straw filled mattress and decided that she would wait no longer. She would make her life what she could, in the village and forget she ever had the run of the palace and gave up believing she ever held the heart of the King in the palm of her hand.

Her face became dull and lifeless, like the coal dust that coated the stacks of metal in the corner. Her beautiful eyes did not shine as much anymore. Mark, the itinerant smith, noticed these things. One day, as she sat staring into the white-hot coals of the forge he asked her, "My Lady, are you unwell? You seem quiet these last days."

She looked at the man standing here in his dirty black apron. "No, I don't feel poorly," she said abruptly. But the truth was that her heart was broken. Her purpose had collapsed because it hung on the love of her Father calling her home. Without his love she felt very poor indeed.

Mark looked around to see if anyone was near. He walked over to Rose. "You know," he said quietly. "I don't understand. You used to carry yourself like a princess. But lately it seems you have become just another villager that is content to stay this way forever. That is not the Rose who gave me this job."

Rose shrugged. "You are mistaken if you once thought I was different to whom I am now. I *am* just another villager. I have become what I was meant to be."

Mark looked away. "Then perhaps my time here is done, because it was you who made me feel that this gave me an opportunity to make a difference."

* * *

Found

Rose stared at Mark as he turned his back. She didn't know what to say or know how she should feel. Why was it always up to her to make a difference? She did not belong here. The villagers who lived here were the ones with the real power to change how things were.

Suddenly she realised. She had acted like a princess because she was a princess. She believed she was a princess... and it showed. Right now – she was still the same princess, but she had lost her belief. She quietly left Mark in the workshop and climbed up the rough ladder to her mattress and pulled out her diary. She read the inscription again...

"To my dearest daughter,

May the lessons you learn

bring more wisdom

than all the learning from many books.

~ from your beloved Father."

Her Father's message had not changed. He had not given a timeframe in which she would stay his *dearest daughter*. He had not limited how long he would be her *beloved Father*. If she believed what he said, his motivation in asking her to undertake this mission was about preparation and acquiring wisdom. He loved her and he didn't want her unprepared. He understood she needed this so she could perform her role in the Kingdom more effectively when the time was right.

Rose felt her heart flutter: she *was* still his princess. Regardless of where she lived, or what she ate, she *was* the daughter of the King. He had given her an assignment that needed her attention. A horrifying thought flicked passed her mind. What if the King called for her today? How shamed she would feel if he asked to see her diary now.

Rose turned to the last page in her diary. She read each item on her list. They all seemed to be impossible things to change. How could she make a difference when they considered her an outsider and a stranger?

* * *

Rose went to the pond with Peggie's laundry and sat watching the ducks. Some other women came with their baskets and water buckets. She joined in their chatter. One mother was talking about her sick children. Another was complaining about the heavy water buckets. Rose listened and sympathised. Then she asked a simple question: "How could we change such a thing?"

A tired sort of laughter dribbled over the scrubbing boards. It was obvious they scorned the idea. This was the way it had always been. Rose slowly dragged over a heavy load of wet washing. "There must be an easier way," she said wistfully.

There was total silence, until one lady spoke up. "Well if you find it, let me know, because my back should surely like an easier way."

That brought another trickle of laughter. They were relaxed now in the impossibility of their static circumstances. But then everything went quiet very suddenly when Rose said, "I've heard that other villages have a well."

Eyebrows arched and then frowned. Surely, she was not suggesting something so outrageous. Finally, a slight, young, newly married bride named Sadie, spoke quietly, "If there was a central well, think of the convenience and time we would save walking down here to the pond."

"Oh yes... I could spend more time on my quilts. It hardly seems fair I only get to work on them when the pond is frozen over." Someone else mentioned those they knew who had shovels and the conversation started to gain momentum as Rose listened with excitement to their dreaming.

Suddenly an older woman spoke up. "Listen to you all," she laughed. "We are not able to do any of this! We don't have the money, or the time, or anything. There may not even be any water there anyway. Why mess with the way things are for something that might not be?"

The string had been tugged too hard and their dreaming-kites fell flat on the ground.

"I don't believe you," said Rose quickly trying to blow up a breeze for the dream-kites to float and fly again. "Why would there be no clean water underground? The village pond is always here. It must be fed by something."

"What would ye know? You can't see such water. We could have dry well holes all over the village and our children will fall into them and die. It's best to leave things the way they are."

The others sighed and were embarrassed at their foolishness. Of course she was right.

Sadie, refused to give up. "I know my Jim would help dig it. I would love to have a well like that in the village square."

The other's laughed. "The honeymooner still has stars in her eyes. Reality will catch up with her soon."

But Sadie did not bend under their teasing. "I don't want reality to catch up with me; especially when it is this hard, ugly reality. I am not strong like you. I have to look for something to change or I will never see any of my babies come or grow to be married. And that is something I want. I'm sure the King would support such an idea."

Rose held her breath, as the laughter grew louder. "Him! His majesty would only want to put a new tax on the well if he found out about it!" they scoffed.

Rose's face grew hot. She did not know why they would say such a thing! "The King would never do that. He loves his people!"

"Him? Ha! We never see him. He never has been here – nor his family! He is comfortable in his tax-sponsored palace."

"No!" cried Rose at the injustice of the claim. "He has sent someone! He has appointed..."

"Who?"

"Someone who is dear to him!"

"Yeah right. I'll believe that when I see it."

"But..." How could she ever explain?

"It's alright dearie. You are obviously used to things being different... but reality is hard and oppressed and ugly. That's life. Even Sadie will get used to it."

* * *

But Sadie didn't get used to it. She became quiet and sad and withdrawn. When Rose asked what was wrong, she started to cry. "Jim and I want so much to start a family, but it seems that we cannot have babies. I still am not pregnant. I don't know what to do. I have eaten all the red clover I can stand."

"Red clover?" asked Rose bewildered.

"Red clover is supposed to help me get pregnant. The midwife said it might help."

"Oh," said Rose. "Well, I know nothing about babies. The midwife would know about such things."

"I just ache to hold a little baby. The midwife said I should learn to help her, so that if I never have my own babies, I can help cuddle other babies. That is what happened to her. I told her I would like to learn, but I will also have my own babies. The midwife liked that. She said I was sassy. Midwives have to be sassy."

Rose smiled. "Sassy Sadie has a ring to it. You will be the best mother-midwife this village has ever had."

Sadie smiled a sad smile. "It will help me wait and be a better mother when my time comes. I will tell the midwife this is what I want to do."

One day, Mark was firing up the forge, and Rose was preparing some jobs for him to work. Suddenly she stopped and said, "I *know* the village needs a well. I don't understand why the people can't see it would do better with one."

Mark did not pause turning the metal in the hot coals. "Better or not, you can't just dig a well by yourself," he said.

"That is not what I meant at all," said Rose. "I will find people who will dig it with me. Sadie has told me her husband will help."

"That's not what I meant either. You just can't go and dig a well, if the people don't want it."

"Why not? If it is a good idea, it is still a good idea whether the villagers recognise it as such, or not."

Mark hammered the hot metal on the anvil most emphatically. "Rose, I know you want to help, but the truth is: it is the villagers who need it, and when they *want* it, they will see that it happens. Then you can help."

Rose grunted in a most un-princess like fashion. "You don't want to help because you are from a different country. You have no heart for these people. You are not really concerned whether their lives are made better or not." She was angry he could not support her idea. Mark looked the other way while he stacked some wood beside the forge. He said nothing. Rose could tell he didn't care.

She turned to Fillip who had just walked into the workshop and asked a question. "Fillip, you have been in the village all your life. Surely you could see the benefit in a well?"

Fillip tied his blackened leather apron around his waist. "Once I believed I did not deserve to have extra rags and bones in my hand cart, because things had always been hard for me. But now I have training from a kind master who wants to teach me a trade. Yet the master is tired and sick, and I fear that I have more to learn than he has time to teach me. If I could change one thing... I would have sick people like him become healthy."

Rose ha-umphed in Mark's direction. See – she was right. "Water from a village well would not have sickness in it. I am sure it would help the people be healthier. But if I have to wait until they decide the well would be an improvement, it will never happen. I can count on one hand the number of people who could believe that such a thing is possible."

Fillip looked at her again. "Once I would have said it was more ambitious than was my right to want my own pushcart. If someone had dared to suggest I would have a *horse* and cart, I would have thought they had moon-sickness. Now I can make carts and save money for as many horses as I need ... and the village is a much cleaner place now because if it. Things that I once thought were preposterous are no longer impossible. Somehow you need to give the people eyes to see what they cannot see."

Mark looked over from where he was hammering on the anvil. "Rose, why do you bother with this? What does it matter to you?"

Rose looked across the smoky forge and her beautiful eyes flashed with anger. How dare he be so careless about the lives of the people in her village! "Mark, I care about the friends I have made. I care that the King's lands have become neglected, and that his people suffer. You will soon leave like all the other itinerants... you use this job as an amusing past-time. But not everyone has that luxury. You will go and they will continue their work, confined by dreamless lives because no one showed them they were allowed to dream, and those dreams could fly."

Mark opened his mouth and closed it again like a fish. He saw that Rose was angered by his remark.

Fillip said nothing more. He hammered out hot metal and doused it in a barrel of cold water, so it sizzled as it cooled. Again and again, he worked the iron, rhythmically hammering as if he was playing a part in a musical minstrel band. Finally, he set his project on the bench where Rose sat calculating some figures. "If the people could see what it is they are missing, then perhaps they would be more willing to support such an idea."

Rose smiled and picked up the work Fillip had placed on the bench. It was a small wishing well.

Now she had a plan. She found someone who could test for underground water using a forky branch from a hazelnut tree. There was water that ran close to the village square. Slowly, Peggie, Fillip and Sadie helped Rose move some stones to build a model of a well. They positioned it where the women passed by every day to go down to the pond outside of the village. She hung a sign that said: *"Well water, free to all villagers"*...

The villagers began to talk. Some asked what the sign said. Some were angry she wrote a sign when she knew the villagers could not read. They said she was showing off. The women would comment as they passed the well-model, "If this was a real well, we'd be finished our chores and on our way home already."

Then someone would say, "What good is a pile of stones? Does she think water is going to come from rocks now? Rocks are more likely, I guess. No one can prove it would really work. We have never had a well in our village before."

And to that another replied. "Not here perhaps, but other villages do. Why should our village be the only place where the people don't have water without sickness in it?"

"What makes you think the sickness in our village is from the water?" they said.

"That's ridiculous... generations have drunk from that duck pond, and they all have families to show for it. We wouldn't be here if it really is the cause of all our sickness."

"The idea is a suspicious one. The King will think we are discontents – rebelling against him. There will be arrests..."

"Better to be free and a little sick, than arrested and end up with our head on a pike."

***

Digging the Well

Rose got up early one morning and went to get some water. The bucket sloshed as she hauled it back to the Blacksmith shop. She rested on the model of the well. The pile of rocks that had become known as a memorial to stupidity. She was angry. Baby Lottie was sick again. How could she get them to understand this would help them? She sighed and guessed that if talking could make a difference she would not be lugging a heavy bucket of water all the way from the pond this morning. Nor would she need to rest on a pile of stones that was supposed to represent the possibilities. She sighed and picked up her bucket and walked slowly home. It started to rain.

When Mark fired up the forge that morning he was distracted. Today was a special day. When he looked around, he was surprised that his jobs were not set out ready. He was irritated because this meant he would not have much work done when Fillip came in from his rounds. Today of all days! Today he needed to finish early. Only a few customers came in, and they were whispering in scandalous tones. They stopped when he looked up from the forge. Mark demanded to know what they were talking about and stared at them viciously until they answered. They wagged their heads and muttered about a riot and a head on a pike in the marketplace.

Mark threw down his apron. He ran through the puddles in the streets and around the huts to the marketplace. There was a small crowd of people in the square huddled in the corner and he pushed his way through. Surely, he could break up the trouble before it got out of hand. But instead of a fight, there was a grubby, muddy little man bent over digging a hole where Rose had built the model well. He smiled to himself. A breakthrough: someone had started digging Rose's well. When he stood up Mark jolted. It was Rose who stood there in overalls knee deep in mud. "Your Highness!" he exclaimed. "What are you doing? Please get out of the mud!"

Rose's jaw fell open. He called her by her royal title. He knew? All this time... and all his remarks... he knew? She remembered that there was rarely a moment when he was not around, always there in the background, even in his careless remarks he became a shadowy protective presence. Suddenly she understood – he was sent by her father. "Please," he said quietly, "Please get out of the mud!"

She lifted her head just slightly. "Mark – if you truly are here for me... then you would not ask me to abandon this. You would pick up that shovel and help me dig."

He considered her for a moment and then quietly nodded. "Yes, your Highness." He picked up a spade and stepped down into the mud and began to shovel. Slowly the crowd got bored and began to disperse.

* * *

Rose paused in her digging and looked at those who were left. Sadie and Jim. Only Peggie and Fillip had joined them. Fillip and Jim were lugging buckets of mud away and dumping them in his cart. Rose smiled as she watched Sadie fuss over Jim and hoped the midwife could help them have a family of their own. Jim was a hard worker, and Sadie was a very caring person, even if she was a bit sassy. Peggie and Fillip had officially announced they were planning to get married in spring. Business was going well with Peggie managing the partnership and now she was teaching her children to read and write. She wanted to be sure that one day they could handle the business well.

As Rose shovelled the mud, she could see that there had been a shift. Ever so slightly and ever so slowly... but she could see a change. It was these few people who had been carriers of that change. They were the weak ones, the village misfits who had not fitted in: a poor rag and bone man; a destitute widow; a sickly, idealistic bride... but these were the sparks for a new, improved way to fire up.

Rose frowned. "Mark – the villagers all heard you call me "Your Highness", yet not one person even questioned it. Do they know?" she asked quietly.

"Oh no. I've kept your secret. I have said it sometimes by mistake. I told those who heard me it was my pet-name for you. They thought that was a little weird, so then I said we are going to be married. Now they think it is cute that you are my princess." He smiled cheekily. "But they are not happy that you have kept this secret of our impending marriage from them. It does not show trust."

She tossed her head at him. "I am sorry they are distressed, but my marriage is not in your hands or mine. That is something my father has arranged. It is a political matter. I have long reconciled myself to such a marriage."

"I know that is so... but if you had a choice, would you mind marrying me?"

Rose stood up and wiped mud across her nose as she brushed her hair back off her face. "Not too long ago I would have said you were the last person I would like to marry. But today you are in the mud, digging a hole in the village square with me. I thought you did not support what I do here, but I think you understand more than I allowed. I would not mind getting to know you more..."

Mark smiled and went back to digging. "It is a shame that it will not happen then."

Rose looked at him digging in the muck. "Yes, it is a shame." And she went back to shovelling out a well in the silence of a village that did not care.

"Ahem. You there! Give an account, sir, of what is going on here!"

They both turned around and looked up in shock. There on a horse sat the Royal Advisor, the King, and behind him a stream of dignitaries that trailed back through the village square. The dispersed village crowd had miraculously reappeared, silenced by the show of the King's guard waving banners, tall lances, and swords.

Mark scrambled out of the muddy hole and bowed low on the cobblestones. "Your Majesty. Welcome to our humble village. As instructed, I am here with the Princess Royal, your daughter."

He turned towards Rose. She stood in the mud, tears streaming down her face, washing tracks down her cheeks. "Father! You came..."

The King dismounted and lifted his daughter from the well. He gave her a long embrace, mud smearing all over his royal robes. "My daughter, this is an interesting look for you. To see this much energy put into a project! You are to be commended."

"But Father, I look a mess. I was not prepared for your visit today. But I could not put this off any longer and still I have not finished. There is so much more that needs to be done! Digging this well is really just the beginning..."

He lifted her chin gently with his hand. "Now, now, I did not say you had to finish... but I did expect you to start. You have many more years of work ahead of you. I would be more concerned if I thought you believed it was all complete and there was nothing more to achieve. Come, show me what your life has been like and where you have journeyed to bring you to the point of digging a muddy hole in the village square this day."

Together they walked back to the Blacksmith shop. On the way Rose took him to the pond and explained why the well was so important. She showed him the clean streets and the new horses in Fillip's stables. She introduced him to the old Blacksmith master and showed him the workshop with the plans for an extension that would become a schoolroom. More space was needed because a woman down the street asked Peggie to include her children in the lessons. She wanted them to read the signs Rose had posted on the well.

Rose introduced her father to Sadie and the midwife and explained how she was in training to become the next village midwife. And last she showed him her little garden with rows of potatoes, turnips and a rose bush. "This has been my favourite project because the rose bush reminds me of home... and home reminds me of you."

Her father smiled. "I gave you a diary my daughter. Show me what you have written in your journal."

"Oh father, please forgive me, I have not filled out the book as you expected... it is not complete."

"Show me, my daughter."

Sheepishly Rose climbed the ladder to the loft and pulled out her diary from under her mattress. She handed it to him. He opened the cover and read to the inscription he had written:

"To my dearest daughter,
May the lessons you learn
bring more wisdom
than all the learning from many books.
~ from your beloved Father."

"Show me the lessons you have learned," he said.

"I have not written them down Father. They are not there."

The King opened the pages and read the few entries. As he went to close the book, the last page flicked open, and he read the list of words written there.

Civil sanitation

Employment

Winter fuel

Health care

Education
Village well

"This is a very comprehensive and challenging list my daughter. I would expect it would take years to implement such a program."

"I do understand that father. In truth I had forgotten about the list. I have not compiled the studies I was supposed to. I have not completed my assignment well," she confessed.

"My daughter, all morning you have been showing me progress on your project list. This is what you have shown me...

Civil sanitation – there is a very effective garbage collection system in place. The village is serviced every day by the rag and bone cart. This is good.

Employment – you have created jobs. Peggie has a shop with apprentices and Fillip has other collectors to help him.

Winter fuel – you supply the village with a reliable source of quality coal at a competitive and fair price.

Health care – there is a new mid-wife in training. You are teaching the children about boiling water before they drink it and growing fresh vegetables in your garden. I know there is more to do, but these are sound grounds on which to start.

Education – Peggie is teaching her children what she has learnt from you. She is including other children from the village in this service. To find another suitable tutor to assist her in this task should not be too hard.

Village well – Well, well... the well. We all know about the progress of the well. The village can spare a few of the workers from the field to help dig this well. If it is good enough for the Princess Royal it is good enough for them.

My daughter, you have done this in the short time you have been here. With what you had... you did well."

Rose sat beside her father subdued. She felt so unworthy for such praise. She had resented the deprivation and the hard work. She had whinged about her circumstances, and her lack of support.

She stopped and looked at her father sheepishly. "Mark helped me more than I gave credit for. I thought he was a disengaged, uninterested apprentice... but I realise now that what I saw was not the whole picture. I was so angry with him."

The King smiled. "Sir Marcus had his own mission to fulfil. His country seeks an alliance. The circumstances of your graduating assignment provided us with a unique opportunity. First and foremost, he was to prove his worthiness by keeping you safe... while staying anonymous. And if he could inspire you to be partial to the idea of marrying him in the time that he was here, I have agreed our kingdoms will align through your marriage. He is the sixth noble who has come seeking your hand in marriage through this quest."

"The itinerants who came to work in the workshop were all suitors?"

"He is the only one who stayed the distance. Now daughter, are you agreeable to his hand?"

"Father, I have understood since I was a little girl that you would organise my marriage. It is a political matter of state."

"Daughter, I would not have you marry against your will, no matter how politically astute. This man is from a noble family. He has done what I asked of him. Now it is up to you."

Rose thought about Mark... Sir Marcus actually, and how he was making up stories in the village about being secretly engaged to her. She thought that very presumptuous. Yet he was the one who was smiling at her as he was digging in the mud. He was used to a privileged life as well. He never complained about his work at the blacksmith shop, or the meagre jobs he was asked to do. He did the garbage rounds on the days Fillip needed him to. And apparently... he could keep a secret. "Father, I am agreeable," she said quietly.

* * *

Happily ever after

Princess Rose and Sir Marcus were married in a magnificent cathedral. Baby Lottie was a flower girl, and Sadie was not able to be an attendant because she was pregnant and could not fit into her dress. Fillip wore a suit and made the most ornate forged iron wishing well for their royal garden as a wedding gift. Peggie cried all the way down the aisle because she could not believe her best friend was a princess and was moving away from the village forever. Rose held the biggest bunch of pink roses in her hand, and she invited the entire village for a feast afterwards.

After their honeymoon, Rose moved to Sir Marcus' Kingdom where she took up a very important political position as Official Ambassador for her father the King. Being the Official Ambassador was a challenging appointment, but in truth, Rose thought that nothing was as hard as...

trusting your father, even when you don't understand...

keeping your heart fixed on his love, even when you can't see him...

and digging in the mud to make where you are a better place, even when no one appreciates you.

Sometimes Rose would just sit by the well in her garden under the foreign moonlight and think of a tiny mattress in the blacksmith loft. Then she would take out her journal and write down more of the lessons she has learnt, that were not found in books.

The End

⌘ ⌘ ⌘

Other books by this author

Matt's Boys of Wattle Creek

Maggie & Minotaur

Gems of Australia Series:
Sapphires of Hope
Rubies of Ambition
Emerald Dreams

Homes of Healing Series:
The Beachside Cottage
Petrea Downs
The Writer's Retreat

Guthrie's Lot Series:
A Spacious Place
A Level Path
The Crying Tree

Pioneers of Grace Series:
Time of Grace
Circle of Grace
Journey of Grace
Mask of Grace
Crucible of Grace
Sculpture of Grace

Children's Book

The Bush Olympics.